Alien Invasion!

Mudpuddle Farm

michael morpurgo

Interior illustrations by Shoo Rayner

Cover illustrations by Cecilia Johannson

Martians at Mudpuddle Farm first published in Hardback by
A&C Black (Publishers) Limited 1994
First published in paperback by Collins, a division of HarperCollins, 1995

Mums the Word first published in Hardback by
A&C Black (Publishers) Limited 1995
First published in paperback by Collins, a division of HarperCollins, 1996

This bind-up edition published by HarperCollins *Children's Books* 2008

HarperCollins *Children's Books* is a division of
HarperCollins*Publishers* Ltd
77-85 Fulham Palace Road, Hammersmith, London W6 8JB

The HarperCollins *Children's Books* website address is
www.harpercollinschildrensbooks.co.uk

3

ISBN-13 978-0-00-727513-7
ISBN-10 0-00-727513-7

Printed and bound in England by
Clays Ltd, St Ives plc

Contents

Chapter One

There was once a family of all sorts of animals that lived in the farmyard behind the tumble-down barn on Mudpuddle Farm.

WAKE UP YOU SLEEPY HEADS

At first light every morning Frederick, the flame-feathered cockerel, lifted his eyes to the sun and crowed and crowed until the light came on in old Farmer Rafferty's bedroom window.

One by one the animals crept out
into the dawn and stretched

and yawned

YAWNNNNNNNN

and scratched themselves.

But no one ever spoke a word – not
until after breakfast.

7

Early one morning old Farmer Rafferty looked out of his window. The corn was waving yellow in the sun. The stream ran clear and silver under the bridge, and the air was humming with summer.

The bees will be out flying today, and that means honey. And honey means money, and I need to buy a new tractor. The old one won't start in the mornings like it should. Get busy bees. Buzz my beauties, buzz!

Chapter Two

Deep in the beehive at the bottom
of the apple orchard, Little Bee was
getting ready for his first solo flight.

And off flew Little Bee out into the wide blue sky. Round and round he flew, looking for the clover field, but he couldn't find it anywhere.

So he buzzed down towards the old
tractor where Mossop, the cat with
the one and single eye, was trying
hard not to wake up.

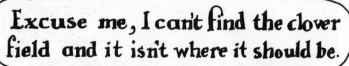

Excuse me, I can't find the clover field and it isn't where it should be.

Mossop opened his eye.

Left at the pond.

Right at the bottom of the field.

Then left again at the blackberry hedge.

Then he went back to sleep again.

The trouble was that Little Bee
didn't know his right from his left
or his left from his right.

Round and round he flew looking for the clover field, round and round till he began to feel giddy

Little Bee felt a great yawn coming on. He looked down for somewhere soft to sleep and then he saw the tractor with the old cat still asleep on the seat.

His tail looks nice and soft and warm. He won't mind, he won't even know I'm there.

And he was quite right about that.
Mossop never even felt Little Bee
land on his tail. He was too busy
dreaming. So Little Bee and Mossop
snoozed together in the sun and the
hours passed.

Chapter Three

Back in the beehive, Queen Bee
was getting worried. Little Bee had
been gone for hours now and
something had to be done.
She called all her bees together.

Right, forget pollen-gathering,
forget honey-making. Little
Bee is lost and we've got to
find him before dark else he'll
get cold and die. Follow me.

Ah-ha!
Once more
unto the
breach!

Old Farmer Rafferty was milking
Aunty Grace, the dreamy-eyed
brown cow, when he heard the bees
coming. 'There they go,' he
chortled over his milk pail.

And then he began to sing as he often did when he was happy.
He sang in a crusty, croaky kind of a voice, and he made it up as he went along.

Honey bunch, be my Queen Bee. Wont you Honey Honey Bee, be my Honey Bee, be my

Great words!

Shame about the tune!

MILK

MILK

Out in the clover field Diana the
silly sheep

was rolling on her back

to scratch her itches

when she saw a great swarm of bees
coming straight towards her.

She struggled to her feet and ran off towards the pond as fast as her legs could carry her. No one was at all surprised when she jumped right in. That's what she always did when there were bees about.

As usual it was Jigger, the almost always sensible sheep dog, who had to pull her out.

'And some mothers do have them,' thought Albertine from her island in the pond.

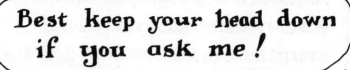

said
Upside
and Down.

So the two white ducks that no one could tell apart upside-downed themselves in the pond and stayed there all day long.

Captain, the great black carthorse who loved everyone and whom everyone loved, looked out over the clover field.

I don't like the look of this at all. There's too many of them and....and they're coming this way!
Do pigs like honey, mummy?
I shouldn't be surprised if they do!

The bees were right over their heads now and they sounded angry, very angry indeed!

DON'T MOVE!

But no one could move anyway.
They were all too terrified, except
Albertine of course.

'Albertine,' said Captain without
moving his lips. 'What are we
going to do?'

Chapter Four

Albertine thought her deep goosey
thoughts for a moment. Then she
said, 'Just follow me'. And she
swam across the pond, waddled
through the open gate and out into
the cornfield beyond.

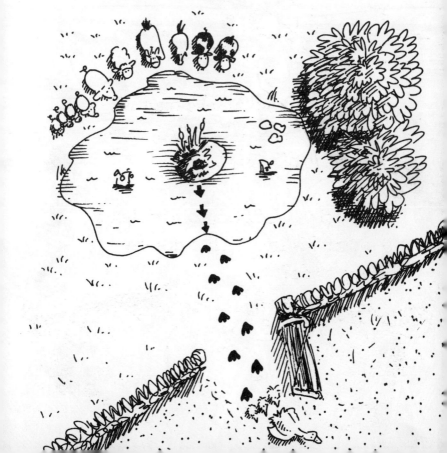

All the animals followed because they knew that Albertine was the most intelligent goose that ever lived. If anyone knew what to do, she would. They reached the middle of the cornfield and looked up. The bees were still following them.

Albertine began to run
round in a great big circle.

All the animals did the same, running round and round and round

And above them the bees all flew round and round and round.

'I wish,' said Aunty Grace,

I wish someone would tell me why we're doing this. The bees aren't going away and I'm feeling giddy.

Me too dear!

said Primrose.

'Good,' said Albertine.

If you're feeling giddy, then the bees are feeling giddy.

She's so logical!

Not many people know this, but when a bee feels giddy, he gets sleepy too; and then he'll buzz off home to sleep. Never fails, you'll see. Keep going.

So round and round they all ran until suddenly the buzzing stopped. When they looked up the bees had all buzzed off, just as Albertine had said they would.

How do you do it?

It's called genius!

She's a wonderful mother too!

And so modest.

Chapter Five

The bees were flying home over the
farmyard when one of them
suddenly spotted Little Bee all
curled up asleep on Mossop's tail.
'Follow me,' said Queen Bee and down they flew.

'I got lost,' cried Little Bee.

I want to go home.

'Soon,' Queen Bee yawned.
She could hardly keep her eyes
open, she was so sleepy.

But first we'll hang about here and have a little snooze.

And so that's what they all did.
Soon there was a great ball of
snoozing bees hanging on
Mossop's tail.

MEANWHILE....

Back in the cornfield, Captain had
a worried look on his face.
'Just look what we've done to
Farmer Rafferty's corn,' he said.
'Just look.' And they looked.

They had flattened out a huge circle in the corn. Not a single solitary stalk still stood standing.

They all heard him. He was
walking into the field singing his
honey song.

honey, oh honey. Won't you be

When Farmer Rafferty reached
the middle of the cornfield, there
wasn't an animal to be found.
What he did find was a great
circle of flattened corn.

Then off he went towards the
farmhouse, counting on his fingers
and muttering to himself.

He didn't know it, but from behind
the farmyard wall the animals were
watching and listening to every
word.

'What's a Martian?' Diana asked and of course everyone looked at Albertine.

'Well,' she said, thinking very hard indeed, 'they walk stiffly like robots do and they carry ray-guns like Farmer Rafferty says.' The animals could hardly believe it, but if Albertine had told them then it had to be true. After all there was nothing Albertine didn't know.

Chapter Six

Farmer Rafferty was still counting
on his fingers when he passed by
the old tractor and noticed the ball
of bees hanging on Mossop's tail.

*Oh dear me. My bees
have gone and swarmed.
Perhaps they couldn't find
the way back home. I'll
have to put them back in
their hive.*

And he disappeared inside the
farmhouse.

While he was gone, the animals
crept back into the farmyard, just
in time to notice something coming
in through the farmyard gate.
It was dressed in white from
head to toe.

It wore a white helmet

and white gloves

and it walked stiffly like a robot,

and as it walked it puffed smoke
out of its ray-gun.

In its other hand it carried
a great big sack.

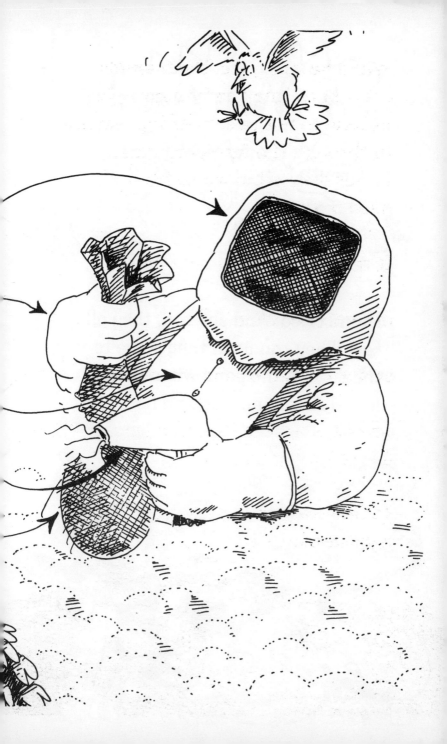

A Martian!

Diana cried. And she ran, they all ran. They ran until they came to the edge of the pond where they found Albertine washing herself.

'It's a Martian,' panted Jigger, the almost always sensible sheepdog.

Albertine smiled her goosey smile.

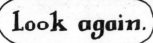

Look again.

That's not Martians, that's Old Farmer Rafferty in his bee-keeping costume. Now watch...

FARMER RAFFERTY

HELMET

SMOKE GUN

SACK

And they watched as old Farmer Rafferty puffed smoke around the swarm of bees.

Puff!

Farmer Rafferty scooped the bees into his sack, and off he went singing his honey song, with Queen Bee and Little Bee and all the others still snoozing inside.

Chapter Seven

Later that afternoon the first cars
arrived. Before long, Front Meadow
was filled hedge to hedge with cars,
and there were people everywhere.
Mossop, who had woken up by now,
walked down the lane and met
Jigger and the others.

It says...

RAFFERTY'S CORN CIRCLE

GENUINE

MARTIAN CORN CIRCLE

To visit .... Two Pounds

Car Park .... Two Pounds

Martian Cream Tea..... Two Pounds

(Honey _not_ Strawberry Jam!)

'No one's going to believe a silly story like that, are they?' said Jigger; but when Albertine looked at him he wished he hadn't said it.

'I think,' said Albertine 'that we believe mostly what we want to believe.'

Chapter Eight

That afternoon Farmer Rafferty showed all the visitors round his Martian corn circle.

After that they settled down on the
front lawn to a Martian cream tea.

He told them the story of the flying
saucer and the Martians that had
landed on Mudpuddle Farm, and
they swallowed it all (the cream
teas and the story) and went
home happy.

And old Farmer Rafferty was happy too. He'd soon have enough money to buy his new tractor.

All red and shiny it would be, with
a proper cab on it so he could
plough his fields without getting
wet and so Mossop could sleep out
of the wind.

But Mossop was quite happy out on the old tractor in the farmyard. None of the animals ever told him about the day the bees swarmed on his tail. They thought it might give him bad dreams, and they didn't want that.

The night came down, the moon
came up, and everyone slept on
Mudpuddle Farm.

Chapter One

There was once a family of all sorts of animals that lived in the farmyard behind the tumbledown barn on Mudpuddle Farm.

You are the sunshine of my life...

At first light every morning Frederick, the flame-feathered cockerel, lifted his eyes to the sun and crowed and crowed until the light came on in old Farmer Rafferty's bedroom window.

One . . . . by . . . . one,
the animals crept out into the dawn . . .

. . . and stretched . . .

. . . and yawned . . .

. . . and scratched themselves.

But no-one ever spoke a word, not until after breakfast.

One morning, Captain was crunching away at his last mouthful of breakfast hay when he noticed something was wrong.

Someone was missing.

Albertine and her little goslings were preening themselves on their island.

Upside and Down
were upside down
in the pond.

Peggoty and her little piglets,
including Pintsize, snuffled and
snorted around the dungheap.

Diana the silly sheep who couldn't
count to save her life, was counting
the clouds.

Penelope and her chicks scratched
and scuffled in the orchard, never
too far from Frederick.

Grace and Primrose grazed nose to
nose in the meadow.

Jigger, the almost always sensible
sheepdog, was chasing his tail again.

And Mossop, the cat with the one and single eye, was curled up asleep on his tractor seat as he always was.

BUT, where was Egbert the grumbly goat?

Jigger, have you seen that grumbly goat?

Nope, I'll have a look shall I?

So Jigger looked and looked.

Egbert wasn't anywhere. He'd done a bunk, buzzed off, gone walkabout.

If anyone knows where he is,
thought Jigger, Albertine will,
because Albertine always knows
everything. So Jigger ran down to
the pond.

Albertine, have you seen
Egbert anywhere? He seems
to have gone missing.

But Egbert did not come back. The animals searched here, there and everywhere for him.

But it was no good, he couldn't
find him anywhere. No-one could
find him.

'I can't think where he's gone,' said
Grace, the dreamy-eyed brown cow.
'Nor me,' said Primrose, who
always agreed with her.

I don't know
where he's gone
either.

'I know, I know,'
said Diana, the
silly sheep.

He's gone
missing!

'Don't worry,' Albertine told her
little goslings.

That goat will be
back, you'll see, around
suppertime I should think.

she's so
reassuring.

Chapter Two

Sure enough, just as Old Farmer Rafferty was giving all the animals their supper that evening, Egbert wandered into the yard, grumbling as usual.

I'm tummy-rumbling hungry. I've hardly eaten all day. Where's my din-dins?

'Egbert, where have you been?' asked Farmer Rafferty in the nasty, raspy voice he kept for special occasions.

I've been looking for you everywhere!

'Worried sick we were,' said Captain, the cart-horse that everyone loved and who loved everyone.

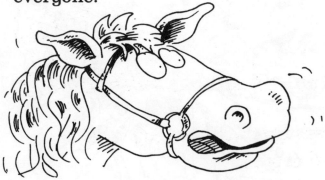

But Egbert wouldn't say another
word about it.

Down on her island in the pond,
Albertine shook her head, smiled
her goosey smile and thought deep
goosey thoughts.

I told you he'd come back, didn't
I? I'll tell you something else too,
just so long as you keep mum,
if you know what I mean. That
goat's been up to something.

what? What? What?

Who knows? Who knows?
Now, let's watch the sun go
down, and then we'll all go to sleep.

Chapter Three

It wasn't long after this that Egbert began behaving very strangely indeed. For one thing, he stopped grumbling. Everyone thought he must be sick, but he wasn't.

Are you feeling all right, Egbert?

Enigmatic Smile

'Good morning,' he'd say as he
passed by,

And he'd say that with the wind
whistling through the farmyard and
the rain thundering down on the
corrugated roofs.

Then one day, Diana the silly sheep
saw something very, very strange.
She saw Egbert dancing! And he
was singing too!

la la la la la

Of course none of the animals
believed her at first, because Diana
was always silly. But she told them
and told them until they had to
come and look.

And of course, when they saw it
with their own eyes they had to
believe it. Egbert was dancing in the
puddles, and singing his heart out.

'He's really sick,'
said Jigger sadly.

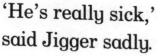

'Hope it's not catching,' said
Penelope, hurrying her chicks away.

'He's gone loopy if you ask me,' said
Peggoty, keeping her distance at the
top of the dungheap.

Mossop opened his one and single
eye and shut it again.

I'm having a bad dream about a singing, dancing goat that's lost his marbles. I think he ought to see a vet.

But Grace and Primrose liked the
song so much that they found a
puddle of their own and joined in.

Albertine sighed and smiled
secretly to herself.

'You'd never understand, Captain,' said Albertine; and Captain felt very stupid.

Captain couldn't understand what Albertine was talking about, but he didn't want to say so in case she might think he was as stupid as he felt he was.

Chapter Four

It was Tuesday, and Tuesday was always the day Old Farmer Rafferty went off to market.

My day out.

He put on his best jacket and his best hat. Then he scooped Mossop off his tractor seat and drove to market.

I'm singing in the hum-te-hum ti tun

Off he went, happy as a lark,
singing to himself as he always did
when he was happy though he could
never remember the words.

I'm singing in the rain, I'm hum ti tum ti tum, what a wonderful hum hum hum

But Old Farmer Rafferty had
forgotten something else, too.
Something much more important
than the words. He had forgotten to
close his vegetable garden gate.

Later that morning, Egbert was
feeling even hungrier than usual.

I've chewed the last of the paint
off the gate. I've eaten the last
of the paper sacks. I've nearly eaten
my rope, but I'm still hungry.

Then he saw Farmer Rafferty's
garden gate swinging in the wind,
squeaking on its hinges.

'Carrots,' he thought. 'Apples.'

No-one saw
him tippy-toeing
out of the farmyard
except Mossop, who
happened to open his one
and single eye as Egbert passed by.

My goat dream
again, only now he's
on his tippy-toes and
ballet dancing!

And he went back to sleep to finish
his dream.

All morning long, Egbert chomped and chewed his way through Old Farmer Rafferty's carrots. No-one noticed what he was up to until after lunch.

Early in the afternoon, Peggoty was taking her piglets for a stroll. As usual Pintsize had run on ahead. That was why he reached the garden gate first. Pintsize knew, and all the animals knew, that none of them (except Mossop because he was special), was ever allowed inside Old Farmer Rafferty's vegetable garden.

Afternoon Mossop.

So when he saw Egbert standing in the middle of the vegetable garden with a carrot in his mouth, he knew that there was going to be trouble, big trouble.

Errk!

Pintsize loved it when other people got into trouble for a change.

Mama! Egbert is in Mr Rafferty's vegetable garden. He's eaten all the carrots!

Peggoty could not believe her eyes.
There wasn't a single carrot left
except the one in Egbert's mouth.

The little piglets gasped. Peggoty let
out her screechiest scream and
called for help.

And all the animals came running
as fast as they could.

'Egbert!' cried Captain. 'Out of there! Out of there! If Old Farmer Rafferty catches you in his vegetable garden your goose will be cooked!' And then he thought about what he'd said.

Oh, I'm sorry Albertine.

munch munch

But Albertine just smiled.

See? I told you Captain, didn't I? Carrots.

But Captain still didn't understand.

'I'll get him out,' said Jigger, the almost always sensible sheepdog. He dashed into the garden and tried to pull Egbert out by his rope. But Egbert would not budge.

Captain came in to help as well but still Egbert dug his heels in and would not move.

Oh come on Egbert. Old farmer Rafferty will be back in a minute.

In fact, Old Farmer Rafferty was just at the end of the farm lane, talking to Farmer Farley from the next door farm. 'Goats,' Farmer Farley was saying, 'who'd have them? They go where they want, eat what they want, do as they please. Still they make you laugh don't they?' And the two of them just laughed and laughed.

Back in the farmyard, the animals all heard Farmer Rafferty coming up the lane on his tractor. He was still singing away.

'I'm off,' said Jigger.

'Me too,' said Captain.

But Albertine decided to wait.
'I think I'll just stay and see what
happens,' she said.

Pintsize hid under Albertine's wings
and pretended to be a gosling.

As Old Farmer Rafferty came through the garden gate, all the animals hid behind the wall and watched.

Suddenly, Old Farmer Rafferty stopped singing. With bated breath, the animals waited for him to shout in his nasty, raspy voice. But he didn't.

All he said was:

You silly old goat, eating all my lovely carrots. Still, I expect you need them more than I do.

And Farmer Rafferty laughed and laughed. He picked up Egbert's rope and led him out into the orchard.

You have all the apples you can find my dear. You'll get fat, but that doesn't matter does it? You eat as much as you like.

The animals could not believe their ears. They could not understand it at all. But Albertine could. She smiled her goosey smile and waddled off back to her pond. Then she climbed up on to her island and tucked her head under her wing and slept. There were four little goslings under her wing that night, and one of them had trotters.

Chapter Five

It turned out just as Old Farmer Rafferty had said. Egbert did get fat, very fat. It wasn't surprising – he did nothing but eat all day long.

He ate anything and everything –

Captain's
best hay,

Jigger's
biscuits,

Peggoty's
pigmeal,

Penelope's
corn,

Diana's
sheepnuts,

and Old Farmer Rafferty's socks off
the washing line.

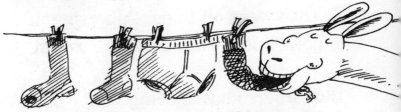

He even ate the sack that Mossop
used for his bed on the tractor seat.
'I'm not dreaming this,' said
Mossop, yawning hugely. 'That goat
is eating my bed.' Mossop was not
at all happy about that.

Right, that's the last straw.
What are we going to do
about that goat?

No-one knew what to do, but they all knew something had to be done. So they went off to ask Albertine. If anyone knew what to do she would.

But Albertine was being very secretive. 'Mum's the word,' she said inscrutably, and she would say no more.

Mum's the word.

what's inscrutable?

Oh!

It means mysteriously unfathomable.

'Well I think that goat needs to lose some weight,' said Grace, the dreamy-eyed brown cow.

And I agree. He's almost as fat as we are, and we are cows. We're supposed to be fat.

But how do you get thin if you're fat?

'Jogging,' said Jigger.

So five times a day all the animals, except Albertine, and all the while Egbert would sing along quite happily, and dance in any puddles he could find. Afterwards they did their aerobics, jogged round Front Meadow. It was all very silly, who thought it was all very silly.

Ridiculous!

'I'm singing in the sun, singing in the sun,' (or rain, depending on the weather). He didn't seem to mind the exercise at all, just so long as he could carry on eating afterwards.

And that's just what he did. He got fatter,

and fatter,

and fatter.

And to everyone's amazement, he stopped grumbling completely. The animals could not believe it.

'I'm just the happiest, luckiest goat in the whole wide world,' he said jumping into another puddle.

'What's he got to be so happy about?' said Jigger. 'What's happened to him?' And he went to ask Albertine again.

But Albertine was keeping mum.
'Mum's the word,' she said
inscrutably, and she smiled a secret
goosey smile again.

Chapter Six

Then one morning, Captain was
looking out of his stable after his
breakfast, when he saw that Egbert
had vanished again.

No-one could find him anywhere.
All day long they looked but they
still couldn't find him.

At last they went to tell Old Farmer Rafferty the bad news.

We've lost him again, we've lost Egbert!

But instead of saddling Captain and going out to look for him, Old Farmer Rafferty just leant on his spade and laughed and laughed.

Why don't you have a look through my sitting-room window?

POW

ZIP

Jigger got there first.

'Oh yes he can,' laughed Old
Farmer Rafferty. 'He can and he
has because *he* is a *she*.
Egbert is Egberta,
and she's just had
two lovely kids.'

And they all peered in at the window. There was Egberta lying out on the sofa, a cushion under her head, with her two little kids beside her.

That evening, Farmer Farley
brought Billy, his billygoat over to
Farmer Rafferty's to see his kids.

'It's my Egberta who's the clever one, bless her,' said Farmer Rafferty.

'I'd say they're both clever,' said Farmer Farley.

Meanwhile, Billy chewed the paint off the window and Egberta chewed the sofa, and both of them looked very happy indeed.

Chapter Seven

Out on the pond, Upside and Down
came up for a breather. 'Anything
new happened?' they asked.

'Not me,' Albertine smiled.
'Egberta. She's the one that's
kidding. It'll be nice to have some
real kids around won't it
children?'

She cuddled her goslings under her wings, including the one with the trotters. 'Do you want a story to send you to sleep?' And of course they did.

The night came down, the moon came up and everyone slept on Mudpuddle Farm.